William Ordway Partridge

The Song-life of a Sculptor

Second Edition

William Ordway Partridge

The Song-life of a Sculptor
Second Edition

ISBN/EAN: 9783744766890

Printed in Europe, USA, Canada, Australia, Japan

Cover: Foto ©Andreas Hilbeck / pixelio.de

More available books at **www.hansebooks.com**

THE

SONG-LIFE OF A SCULPTOR

BY

WILLIAM ORDWAY PARTRIDGE

AUTHOR OF "THE TECHNIQUE OF SCULPTURE,"
"ART FOR AMERICA," ETC.

SECOND EDITION

BOSTON:
ROBERTS BROTHERS.
1895.

University Press:
JOHN WILSON AND SON, CAMBRIDGE, U.S.A.

I DEDICATE these verses to the quickening of that new order of living when men shall be actually free.

For, notwithstanding our boasted emancipation, we are but bondsmen so long as our spirits, and the child-heart within us, are enslaved by tradition, convention, and meaningless forms. We are still living in the shows of things. Freedom is a word upon the lip, not an inspiration for the heart. Those who are in command think themselves free, not knowing that the first element in freedom is obedience. Epictetus, while a slave in body, was actually more free than those he served, and whose bodies could be moved from place to place.

I do not understand why we should not attain the best we are capable of having and being. This would seem to be the truest Political Economy.

May God hasten the time when human life shall be made entirely free and beautiful! Then insight and foresight shall take the place of dogma and authority. Then love shall be the law of life, and poetry its language.

WILLIAM ORDWAY PARTRIDGE.

CONTENTS.

CONTENTS.

SONG–LIFE OF A SCULPTOR.

———•———

KEATS.

CIRCLED by far faint rings of amber light,
　　The moon rides high through drifting silver sprays
That from her beauty fall as garments white
From a lone goddess of the Phidian days.
I dare not sleep, for beauty of these skies :
See, through the drifting cloud the midnight sinks
Deep as the soul of God.　My passion dies
In the pure loveliness my spirit drinks.

This night was made for Keats.　Swooning in light,
With songs too sweet for earth pent in his heart,
Beyond the morrow's pain and petty slight,
His soul and sense at last were borne apart,
Caught upward to the midnight's brightest star :
My spirit, panting, follows him afar.

MID-OCEAN.

IS there no symbol of the land to be,
　　No broken, struggling branch, no floating weed,
Nothing to break the grim and solemn greed
Of this unending, deep-hued, awful sea?

Brave ship to sail upon the unknown track!
Brave hearts that dare, brave souls that longing wait!
Though storm and wind assail, Ship, turn not back:
Let us go on, with faith o'er-topping fate.

How fearful is this scene! Yet many a time
In London town I 've known an hour more drear;
Amid starved souls, and faces dark with crime,
Have felt such heart-ache as one knows not here.
What loneliness akin to that white stare
Of hungry faces, hurrying — God knows where?

TWO WORLDS.

TWO shadows steal along the mountain path,
    All ghostly in the slow and silent wake
Of man and child.   No earthly voices break
The breathless breathing that the spirit hath !
The man's strong hand makes light the weary way,
And something from the child's faith seems to take.
They love each other for love's purest sake,
And hallowed are the twilight and the day ; —

But yesterday these shadows lingered here,
And still the sweet young moon o'er woodland glades
Is moving on ; but now one shadow near,
One only, lingers in the land of shades :
The child alone toils up the mountain height,
But still — two shadows mingle with the night.

SYMPATHY.

OH, let the tendrils from thine inmost life
    Reach deeper still into the human heart!
Then, as the pine upon the far-off hills,
That sent its living roots into the earth,
Is folded soft in purple majesty,
So shall a kindred glory compass thee;
Thy life must glow with this communion. Then
No torrent's shock will shake thy deep-plunged roots;
The world's rough winds will beat upon thy brow,
Only to sink in far-off melodies;
A glory shall invest thee as the stream
Of life upon the bosom of its rest
Bears thee, to mingle with the sunset skies.

COURAGE.

BE not discouraged at thy doubt, O soul !
    Perchance it is the hand of God that leads
Thy faith to nobler creeds and broader trust.
Part of thy manhood is to doubt and solve,
And rise to higher things.   For cobwebs hang
About the intellect as in a court
But little used, and we must let the sun
Pour in and fight and conquer mirk and mist.
The creed thy father built, wherein his soul
Did live, and move, and find its meed of joy,
May be but small to thee.   Then, without fear,
Build o'er again the atrium of thy soul —
So broad that all mankind may feast with thee !

SOWING TO THE SPIRIT.

I F thou hast struck one blow for liberty,
 Be it of slave or shackled intellect,
Thou hast not failed. If into some lone life
The light of nobler days has come through thee,
Flooding the shadowed years with sympathy;
Or if some soul of moral vision dim
Has, through thy love, been led to clearer things, —
Thou hast not failed. If thou hast given a meaning
To flowers that yesterday were set aside,
And clothed them with the beauty of thy thought;
If to hard-handed labor thou hast made
Sweet with enduring rest the twilight hour,
Or shown the beauty of the field and sky
Unto the peasant, or across the wave
Unto some brother thou hast stretched a hand
Amid the oft deceiving tides of life, —
Thou hast not failed. Or if alone thy lot
To find thine own deep faults, and feel the need,

The ever present need of prayer, and faith
In men and things divine, thy life has been
Of more enduring worth than that of kings,
Princes, and prophets of the earth.   The world,
Alas, is but the world.   Hold it at naught,
And do not soil thy sandals with its dust,
Or leave them still without the temple gate !
Undaunted, yet with calm humility ;
Thy sympathy still deepening with thy years —
And past the bourn of failure or success —
Enter in peace the kingdoms of thy soul.

MEMORIES.

THE child still plays on the meadow,
    There 's a glory on the sea,
But my summer is lost in the memories
I hold in my heart for thee.

For to me it was summer only
By a certain gentle grace,
That all things caught, on land and sea,
From the beauty of thy face.

THE WATER-LILY.

DOWN where the alders tremble,
　　By the shimmer and glint of the stream,
I watched a lily awaking,
　　Slow from a stately dream.

I bathed my soul in her beauty —
　　Fair as a queen of old —
Clad in a spotless raiment,
　　Crowned with a crown of gold.

But lo ! when the shadows deepened,
　　Under the fading light,
She gathered her petals about her,
　　And veiled her heart from the night.

And the stars grew weary with watching,
　　And the night-wind sighed o'er the place,
But no more to my spirit was given
　　That vision of beauty and grace.

THE WATER-LILY.

Down where the alders tremble,
   By the shimmer and glint of the stream,
I wait till my lily shall know me
   And wake from her stately dream.

WHERE WAITS A LOVING BREAST.

WHY journey further, weary one?
　　Still fades the sunset-sky;
And many wander all their lives
　　And broken-hearted die.

Then throw aside thy weariness
　　And take this proffered rest,
Where one low light is burning bright
　　And waits a loving breast.

AFTER THE STORM.

AFTER the furious gale of yesternight,
   Who would have dreamed the sea could be so
      fair?
Then waves like jagged rocks tore through the air,
And the wild sky joined in the sea's delight
(Oh, God, how set grew every face, and white !)
To strike the ship, driven we knew not where,
Like some poor hunted thing, in helpless flight
Before a power that heard no human prayer.

And now — the sea lies calm ; the moon, full-round,
Pours quiet splendors o'er the jewelled deep ;
" All 's well," the sailor shouts, — oh, welcome sound,
For weary souls to-night is blessed sleep.
How like to passion in the human breast, —
That tears itself, till love brings holy rest.

A PAINTING BY SÉGÉ.

HOW·great is art when it can grasp and wrest
   The eternal murmurs from the hoarding sea,
The sunset glory from the fading west,
   And bring its solemn grandeur here to me ;
Give back the cool winds to an aching brow,
   The peace of rich dark shadows deep and strong,
The free delight that lifts my tired heart now
   In listening to yon red-capped fisher's song.

How great is art, how great is man, what soul
   Must burn in that frail form, in one short hour
To make that cliff to stand, that sea to roll,
   That sky to smile forever by his power,
Those waves that rise to break for evermore
Across this brave brown rock and trembling shore.

TEACH ME, DEAR HEART.

TEACH me, dear Heart, to love the simple things
    That make the world more beautiful each hour;
That I may speak the tender word that brings
    A smile to lips so wholly in my power;
Let me not keep for those I love the dead
    Dull commonplace exchange of wants and cares,
While for the thankless world my best is said, —
    The world that heeds not how my spirit fares.

Childlike and guileless even to the end,
Trusting each one and smiling as I go,
Finding perchance in every home a friend,
And loving all who greet me here below, —
So let the story of my life unfold
Till twilight closes and the tale is told.

A SUMMER DAY.

WITH nothing to do but to dream and dream,
   As I follow the course of the idle stream,

And the careless thoughts of a summer day —
Light as the thistle-down blown away,

I could live for aye in this idle trance,
My heart as light as a naiad's dance.

I would not change my summer day
For a royal robe and a regal sway,

With nothing to do but to dream and dream,
As I follow the course of the idle stream,

And the careless thoughts of a summer day —
Light as the thistle-down blown away.

BY THE RIVER AT NIGHT.

THE light of the river, the shadow that mars,
By the gloom of the arches, the gleam of the stars ;

The mist that seems hanging and winging for aye
As a ghost or a dream in the wake of the day,

In seasons of pleasure, in seasons of blight,
I walk by the river, the river of night ;

And the burdens of care and the fardels of pride —
They drop from my spirit and sleep in the tide.

ASLEEP.

LONG ago a little sister,
    Bowed beside my knee in prayer,
And she seemed an angel kneeling
    As I touched her golden hair.

Lo ! there came another angel
    From beyond the dusky deep ;
And as bends a flower at evening
    So my sister fell asleep.

SLEEPLESSNESS.

O YE who sleep a care-forgetting sleep
    On sweet home-pillow, or if ocean-tossed;
And hide yourselves in solitudes so deep
That every tumult of the world is lost, —
Belovéd of the Lord, indeed, what bliss
Is yours to wake refreshed and free from pain;
To greet the tender morn's awakening kiss,
And rise new-born with power in heart and brain!

Alas! we watch the day fade into night;
The glory of the stars a sweetness brings,
But no repose until the dull gray light
We shut away, — to dream of troublous things.
God's will be done! We know, though sleep forsake,
Rest comes at last which no world's care can break.

THE CUP OF LIFE.

DRINK deep of life before thou seek to drain
  The last dull cup of cool and liquid death;
Drink every drop, let no rich glint remain
While yet we kiss the brim with eager breath.
The hour-glass runs away with youth and age —
Too quick the sands of life are slipped and crossed;
With trembling hand Time turns another page,
And our slow feet upon the way are lost.

Drink deep of life, — of love's great joy and pain, —
Be king of the swift hours, and not their slave;
Our souls are tempered by the cups we drain
To stronger life and love more strong to save.
Drink deep of what endures, then strangely sweet
Will seem the cup Death brings with lingering feet.

RESIGNATION.

PALE Mother, weep not for the spirit fled ;
　　The face that smiled upon thee with the light
Will greet the angels ere the coming night ;
Nor question God for this, thy darling dead.
The little feet in gentler ways are led ;
The paths of Heaven are more than jasper bright.
His day was but a promise of delight ;
A larger heart than thine pillows his head.

To-night diviner cradle-songs he hears, —
Sweeter than yesterday's.　Why dost thou weep?
Nor will he know the tempests of the years,
But by the Shepherd's side shall gladly keep.
Behold through deepest gloom thy light appears ;
He is not dead who on God's breast doth sleep.

LONGING.

COME back into my heart, its doors await
　　To shut you in, love ; linger not too long,
But come and claim my soul's impassioned song
I hold in trust for you — through some kind fate.
Come, love, with your sweet peace, for it grows late,
Come back, for you are right, the great world wrong,
Come back with your strong faith to make me strong,
To banish doubt and discontent and hate.

Come back to fill my life with truth, thy dower,
As heaven is filled each day with radiant light ;
For love that looks not to itself hath power
To conquer moods that dim the spirit's light.
Come back into my heart ; each lingering hour
I call and call throughout the deepening night.

THE BRITTANY COAST.

SÉGÉ.

THERE stands a rocky cliff, wave-beaten, vast,
  And towering seas break ever at its base,
The abode of life and death, the future, past,
The living sea-weed and the pale dead face;
Above it, stormy sea-gulls wheeling rise
And unaffrighted ride its rugged crest;
I hear them calling now with piercing cries,
While the sun's lingering glory dyes the West.

'Tis but a picture — yes, an image wrought
In massive lines — broad sweeps of color thrown
Over it all by some fine hand that caught
Its wondrous cunning from the vast Unknown;
'Tis but a picture, yet I rest my soul
On those deep tones which the great waves uproll.

THE SPIRIT OF SONG.

S HE has come to the West in the waning light —
    The Spirit of song —
To seek her lover, the peace-crowned Night,
    And tell him the weight of her burden of wrong ;
The white gulls kiss her with whiter wings,
As she sinks in the depths of the pines and swings,
    For her flight was long.

In the murmuring depths of the pines she sinks
    With her weary wings,
And the sunset's purple she drinks and drinks,
    Till her beauty reels as she swings and swings,
And the Night sweeps up on the tide from the West,
And folds her close to his brave, dark breast,
    And is glad and sings.

And the stars grow faint in their watch and still ;
    They listen and pray,

Till the eager lover shall have his will;
    She has waited his coming the long, long day,
Has waited his kiss on her forehead white;
Then kiss her again, O star-crowned Night
    In thine own brave way.

THE BROOK.

L AUGHING, leaping,
  Never sleeping.
    Laughing, leaping thro' the day.
Singing over
Mead and clover,
    Over clover on its way.

Hear it teaching,
Softly preaching —
    Preaching, teaching to the rose,
Songs of beauty
And of duty,
    Duty, beauty, as it flows.

Ever fleeting,
To the meeting —
    Fleeting, fleeting, on it speeds
To the river
All a-quiver
    With its glistening, listening reeds.

And the stilly
Water lily,
    Fragrant lily of the streams,
Bends to hear it
And to cheer it,
    Hear and cheer it as it dreams.

Ever roaming
Toward the gloaming —
    Foaming, foaming in its flight,
Till it pillow
'Neath the willow
    On the bosom of the night.

TWILIGHT.

ON the mountains the shadows linger,
  And the sky is dashed with light,
Tho' the day, that is weary, yieldeth
  Its place to the eager night.

On the mountains the shadows deepen,
  'Neath the tender evening skies;
But no more is their beauty imaged
  In the light of thy lifted eyes.

PARTING.

THE light of the morn is breaking,
   Across the widening sea —
But the glory is dimmed with sadness,
   Sweet love, when I think of thee.

Would it were dark and dreary,
   And a mist upon the brine,
And I were standing near thee
   With thy dear hand in mine.

THE ARC OF SELF–CONTROL.

ONE by one, from the clouds that hurry
　　Across the brow of the storm,
Are the mystical colors gathered
　That gleam in the rainbow's form.

One by one, from the eager passions
　That darken the poet's soul,
Are the deep-toned colors blended
　In the arc of self-control.

FOR A STATUE OF SHAKESPEARE.

WHO models thee must be thine intimate —
    Nor place thee on a grand, uplifted base,
Where tired eyes can hardly reach thy face.
For others this might serve ; thou art too great.
Who sculptures thee must grasp thy human state,
Thine all-embracing love must aim to trace, —
Thy oneness with the lowliest of the race.

Until this sculptor comes, the world must wait ;
But when he comes, carving those deep-set eyes,
'Neath brow o'erarching, like the heavens' high dome,
The men will turn aside with glad surprise
And say, slow-wending from their toil toward home,
" I saw this Shakespeare in the street ; he seemed
A man, like you or me, howe'er he dreamed."

A FRAGMENT.

I WATCHED it grow, the statue from the stone;
  I watched the man with ever patient hand
Caress the marble with as gentle care
As one would touch the form he holds most dear;
And as the stone grew more and more to live
The sculptor seemed to grow away from life.
As a bright chrysalis wears through its rough,
Warm garment, so his soul was wearing fast
The stubborn clay that clogged and compassed it.
Ideal forms of beauty he had seen —
First in his soul, then evermore in dreams —
Grew into being as his thought took form.

I looked into her eyes, those dark, deep eyes
So fathomless that one seemed pausing on
The brink of love's eternity; while she
Divined my thought because the tears would fall
From her long lashes down unto her breast,
Seeming to find some consolation there;

A FRAGMENT.

Then she would lay her head upon his arm
To tempt him from his work : " Beyond the bridge
The Arno flows in pulsing golden light.
Then let us leave our toil, for it grows late,
And wander out upon the purpling hills,
And watch the evening steal along the sky."

SCULPTURE.

ETERNAL peace enthroned upon thy brow
    Looks out across the ages with a faith
Which conquers doubt and cannot know a fear:
The light of some lost vision seems to fall
From thy calm presence, till I wonder where
My soul has known thy soul. At last I trace
Thy beauty back to God from whence it came;
No sin has touched thy stately purity.
Thou lovedst Phidias, it hath been said,
And he alone possessed the peace that falls
Forever from thy calm eternal form;
And knowing thee, he walked through life serene,
Like some one in a dream who sees the steps
Which lead to far-off stars, and evermore
Is glad and smiles, though shadowed be his life,
While men with wonder look upon his face,
Not seeing that bright light which burns within.
And still they whisper in the Parthenon: —

"This sculptor in a dream has talked with God."
His voice, deep-toned and crystal-clear and strong,
Speaks to the sculptor, silent at his task :
"Live one grand love, and living so be glad ;
It is the first and last, the crown of life,
For life is love, and love alone is life,
And love is God, and God alone endures.
Into the shadow from the light thy path
Must lead, O Sculptor Soul, and though thine eyes
Grow dim with tears, the darkness cannot blind,
If thou still cling unto that inner light
Which once hath flooded thee with perfectness.
Be patient, Sculptor, let thy statue grow,
As grows thy life, that both may stand unveiled
Before the very presence of thy God.
Thine is the clearer vision ; the nobler life
Be thine ; cling not unto the passing show ;
It soon is gone.   The type alone endures."
He spake no more with men.   Then Sculpture slept
For countless years too sorrowful to speak.
Asleep she lay till Angelo awoke
Her dreaming beauty, and she rose again.
To all who work in clay he nobly saith :
"Be strong, O artist soul."   With love and toil
He lived and loved and taught and wrought and died

SCULPTURE.

Then Sculpture, leaning on Death's mighty arm,
Bereft of him fell fast asleep again.
And still she sleepeth, waiting for the touch
Of love like theirs upon her silent life.

SPRING IN FLORENCE.

THOU art in Florence, love ; wilt linger there
    Until thou meet the Spirit of the place?
Its streets have looked on Dante's pain-carved face
And trembled at Savonarola's prayer.
There's something holy in the very air,
Something sublime ; a noble, stately race
Made it their home. I do not know a place
In all the world so marvellously fair.

Go where one will, one cannot be alone ;
A train of ghosts is passing every court ;
One treads on history in every stone,
And all art's treasures come to us unsought ;
Dear city of great souls, thy blessing still
In other climes works out its holy will.

VESUVIAN SKIES.

IS there a land, far off, where all things take
   Their tint from skies like these where love lives
     on, —
Infinite, vast, as these Italian heavens
That arch me in from everything but peace?
Near by is Vergil's rest, the wave beyond ;
The lute-voiced Tasso felt what now I feel,
And wove it into lays, — lays not for kings
Who pass away, but lays for man, who runs
With time, and wins the crown — eternity.
Man, the immortal part of kings, he sang ;
So in these later times would I sing, too ;
For still the hours are rich with manly deeds,
That call for song and chide me while I sleep
Upon the bosom of the Infinite.

A RHAPSODY.

AFLOAT, afloat,
   In my tiny boat,
Joyous and free as the emerald tide,
I am steering away
From the gates of day,
Where beautiful, shining sea-nymphs hide.

I rise and fall
At the billows' call
On the breast of the restless, foamy sea;
Yet why need I fear
When the maiden dear
Is fearlessly floating afar with me?

The moonlight plays,
And its silver rays
Dance o'er the maiden who sits on the prow,
While the sweet wind blows
From the Land of Snows,
And softly kisses the Lover's brow.

A RHAPSODY.

Oh ! this is the joy,
With never alloy, —
To snatch a kiss from the mermaid's cheek,
To catch the pearl
That the laughing girl
Drops from her lips as she turns to speak.

Now list ! — they sing
To the Ocean King,
As, far on the billow, they beckon to me ;
And my pulses chime
To the sea-nymphs' time,
As loving, dreaming, I float o'er the sea.

ON THE QUAY AT NAPLES.

ALONE on the quay in this mystic light,
  Alone in the moon's cold rays, —
The free wild thoughts that come to-night
  Are thoughts of bygone days.

I passed thee, love, in a crowded street,
  When my face was wan with care ;
Thy sweet dark eyes sought out my soul,
  And left their glory there.

And when a beggar touched my hand
  I threw him a golden ring ;
For thy beauty seemed so rare a gem
  That gold was a paltry thing.

That night I held thee in dreamy dance,
  Where of all thou wert the queen ;
Thy grace was like a shining star,
  Moving and yet serene.

And away I led thee that very hour,
  Away from the banquet's light
Amid the roses I told my love —
  Sweet love, on that first sweet night.

Oh, the wild, wild burst of passionate grief
  When I found thee a plighted wife !
I looked on death, but I could not leave
  Thy face, for it promised life.

Some loves there are that grow through years,
  But some take sudden birth,
As swift as the midnight meteor's flame,
  Uniting the sky and earth.

Alone on the quay I walk to-night,
  In the moon's mysterious rays,
And the free, wild thoughts that dim my sight
  Are the thoughts of bygone days.

DROWNED.

" HE was a dreamer; 't is well he is dead! "
    This was the eulogy spoke o'er his head.
Scorning your pity, he needs not a tear —
Never had mortal so noble a bier,
Never had monarch so grand a repose,
Never were " yales " so solemn as those;
Even the storm-winds took up the dirge,
Bearing the requiem over the surge:
" Poverty, poverty clung to his wings,
Kept him from soaring to heavenly things.
Fated to fight in the front of the strife,
Chafed by the harness and weary of life,
Nothing was left but the bountiful wave
Giving him freely the grace of the grave.
Think of the peace he had sought for in vain —
Found in the ebb of the fathomless main.
Oh! how he welcomed the chill of thy breath!
Merciful, pitiful, Angel of Death."

THE CONVENT TOWER.

TO the vespers sweetly timing
  Soft and slow the bells are chiming,
    On the air ;
Not a sound the stillness waking,
Save a nun's lips faintly breaking
    Into prayer.

Now my restless heart is sleeping,
Hushed my thoughts, in solemn keeping
    With the time,
While my spirit, beauty drinking,
Marks the swelling and the sinking
    Of the chime.

Ancient belfry, yonder lifting,
Where the purple clouds are shifting
    In the sky,
Through all shine and sunless weather
We have many thoughts together —
    Thou and I.

When the lustrous stars are glowing,
All the welkin overflowing
   With their light,
Then their realms of love they people
With the dead beneath thy steeple,
   In the night.

A SERENADE.

SOFTLY her silken hammock
　　Is rocked by the breezes there;
Gently the moonbeams tremble
　　In the waves of her golden hair.
Hushed be the plaintive murmur
　　Of my silver-voiced guitar,
For the song that to dreamland wooes her,
　　Alas! is sweeter far.
Sleep on, my lovely lady,
　　While the stars their watches keep;
Thy lover will guard thee ever —
　　Sleep on, my lady, sleep!

TO WHOM THE PRAISE.

IF to outlive me, in the coming days,
    I shall have carved some holy thought in stone,
It will be thou, love, and not I alone,
As men may think, to whom is due the praise.

O watchful love, perfected through much pain,
Wooing to rest lest I o'erreach my strength,
Intent upon my work, — thou com'st at length
Softly to stay my hand, and say again : —

" How sweet it is without these prison walls !
What shadows on the hills, what flowery fields,
Await us!" At thy voice my tired heart yields
And I go out to breathe — before night falls.
Ah ! hadst not thou looked further than my eyes,
I had not lived to joy in these glad skies.

IN THE DESERT.

A FERTILE spot in desert land,
Emerald in ring of golden band,
Circled by miles of glittering sand,
Held up a palm as with tender hand.
Strong in its youth, the tree looked straight
Toward heaven, and oft it kindly shaded,
The wandering Bedouin, lost and jaded,
Who thither strayed, as the long day faded,
Thanking his restful fate.

A caravan halting there by night,
Shining with jewels and tinsel bright,
Turning the darkness into light,
Dazzled the quiet palm-tree's sight.
'Wildered — forgetful of purer Eves —
Under the wings of night he wrested
A kiss from a maiden silver-crested,
The pride of the Harem, softly nested
In sleep beneath the leaves.

55

The caravan left at break of day,
And watching them slowly wind away,
Hour after hour, the date-trees say,
He turned his eyes to the western ray.
  Crooked it grew, and bent to the west,
Till at last an Arab pilgrim strayed,
And, fainting, fell beneath the shade,
And there his tranquil couch he made,
    Grateful for dreamless rest.

At dawn he saw, with saddened eye,
The tree so strangely turned awry,
And twined a vine that grew near by
To cling and grace and beautify —
  Nearer and dearer, with tendrils fine
As gently as the turtle-dove,
Soft cooing in the boughs above,
Repeats her plaintive tale of love,
    Oft whispering, " Thou art mine."

Thus sweetly she won him, with loving prayer,
Back from the world of glitter and glare ;
And the palm, with benediction rare,
Bent over the vine that was clinging there.

IN THE DESERT.

Having known the world for a single night,
A wanderer once from early grace,
He never regained his stately place ;
Yet something lovely in his face
  Still makes the desert bright.

IMMORTALITY.

WHAT need of miracle or sign,
  To verify the word divine?
The Power that makes thy senses free
To grasp the thought — Eternity ! —
That Power, if thou but think again,
Can crystallize thy daring brain ;
And while thou think'st to live for aye —
Behold, it breaks — immortal day !

TWO SCULPTORS.

H E passed my way, — the mighty sculptor Death, —
    And looked upon my work with many a frown;
Upon my brow I felt his solvent breath
And stretched my hand to stay his silent gown;
But he was gone, his threat remained alone,
As echoes will outlive the voice that calls:
" Turn thy poor clay till I turn thee to stone,
To lie with folded hands in my vast halls."

Thou boaster, Death, work out thine own dread tho
Till clay and sculptor pay the final debt.
Despite thy vaunt my task shall still be wrought,
From whitest dream in whitest Parian set;
Then 'twixt us twain let God Himself decide, —
Thee who hast mocked and me who have defied.

LIFE'S FRETFUL COMMONPLACE.

A VOICE within me murmured : "Song is dead ;
No more above Life's fretful commonplace
Toward beckoning stars she lifts her royal head,
And thrills my soul to some diviner grace ;
Thy song is dead.   Each hour a galley-slave
Must toil at his low bench with straightened knee,
Nor pushing a slow oar into the wave
Can he forget that once his heart was free."

Dissatisfied I pass into the street,
To find a horse who strives against a hill
Too steep, with bleeding mouth and broken feet.
" My God ! " I cry, " how selfish are we still,
Silent and dumb ; while cruel wrongs await
A saving voice here at one's very gate ! "

IN MEMORY OF MY OLD MASTER.

AH, place no stone above his quiet rest,
   The earth bears now too heavy on his breast.

His love was such a living part of me,
That now 't is gone, my love forgets to be.

Yon stone shall die, as dies our passing breath ;
Both man and marble own the power of death.

The soul alone lives on from age to age,
To bear his name on its immortal page.

No marble raise, but these sweet blossoms lay
To breathe their perfume on the passing day.

And at some twilight hour I 'll steal afar
From lower things that peace and beauty mar,

To watch these tender buds unfold and bloom,
As doth his spirit from the sullen tomb.

Should dew or rain-drop, faithless, fail with years,
This rose might flourish with my sacred tears.

No deed but this proclaim above the sod :
He led a mortal nearer unto God.

A DEAD POET'S SONGS.

SPEAK low ! With tenderest feeling turn this page !
    An ever-burning censer swingeth near ;
For thoughts are prayers and mount to heaven from
        here ;
Immortal love that knows not change or age,
Gave these sweet thoughts our sorrows to assuage.
The fretted brook flows bright beyond the weir ;
My troubled spirit drops its care and fear, —
Nor longer chafes and bruises 'gainst the cage.

The heavens have deepened 'neath his wondering eyes,
Until the young moon's path becomes our own ;
From time we mount into eternal skies,
And he is lifted to his thought-won throne.
Soon he will call, and the earth's twilight dim
I shall put off, and put on light with him.

HER life was like the flow of a calm stream,
    That leaves its peace, where whitest lilies dream,

To turn in dusty towns the toiling mills,
And bear them strength and hope from its brave hills,

Where weary mothers come with faltering steps,
To drink repose from its melodious depths, —

With flow as sweet, where endless strife is made,
As when it leaves its peaceful alder-glade.

Such was her life, as calm, majestic, fair, —
A precious symbol of our Father's care.

Once on that peaceful tide I cast my pain,
And, when I looked, I found it not again.

THE MASTER'S WORK.

THE hands that do God's work are patient hands,
    And quick for toil, though folded oft in prayer;
They do the unseen work they understand
And find — no matter where.

The feet that follow His must be swift feet,
For time is all too short, the way too long;
Perchance they will be bruised, but falter not,
For love shall make them strong.

The lips that speak God's words must learn to wear
Silence and calm, although the pain be long;
And, loving so the Master, learn to share
His agony and wrong.

BROKEN.

OUT of the light, the splendor,
  There cometh a sudden start,
'T is the lyre that, weary of bending,
Has broken its burdened heart.

Out of the sunlit heavens,
Falls a bird with a broken wing,
Hushed is the lyre forever,
And the bird will never sing.

THY WILL BE DONE.

THY will be done through all life's change and chance ;
    No matter if my work find blame or praise ;
With spirit fixed on thee, no circumstance
Shall alter love through life's confusing maze ;
In outward grief let inward joy begin,
    Till life without be lost in life within.

IN MEMORIAM.

CAPTAIN WILLIAM T. PARTRIDGE, KILLED AT GAINES'S MILL,
June 27, 1862.

WITH solemn tread
 Approach this bed
  Where thousand banners wave.
Forbear to weep
O'er such a sleep, —
  It well becomes the brave.

No marble raise
With storied praise, —
  Leave noble deeds alone ;
For Honor's guest
Can calmly rest
  Without the sculptured stone.

Above that shrine,
Almost divine,
  Still bow thy head in prayer,

The noblest deed,
The grandest creed,
 Of man is pictured there.

Along the street,
With muffled beat,
 Where thousand banners wave,—
Forbear to weep
O'er such a sleep;
 It well becomes the brave.

TO PIO WELONSKI, SCULPTOR, ROME.

WHY do men carve these images of stone?
  Is it for those who stare and flock about?
There are, alas! who carve for those alone,
Dependent on the world's approving shout.

But some, whose life it is thro' flying days
To wrest from that rude stone the truth that waits,
Carve dumbly on, nor ask for human praise,
Knowing the God within still compensates.

CHANGE.

THE dearest things in this fair world must change ;
    Thy senses hurry on to sure decay ;
Thy strength will fail, the pain seem no more strange,
While love more feebly cheers the misty way.
What then remains above the task of living?
Is there no crown where that rude cross hath pressed?
Yes, God remains, His own high glory giving
To light thy lonely path, to make it blest.

Yea, God remains, though suns are daily dying, —
A gracious God, who marks the sparrow's fall ;
He listens while thine aching heart is sighing ;
He hears and answers when His children call ;
His love shall fill the void when death assails, —
The one, eternal God, who never fails.

THE FRIENDLY STARS.

WITH weary feet I passed the city wall :
    The night was near, the mountains far away ;
And, as the glow of that blown rose, the day,
Too beautiful, was blushing to its fall,
I paused to rest, — the night was over all.
Lo ! one by one, from out her darkling cloak,
The bright-eyed children of the sky awoke,
And answered, gleaming, to my silent call.

The stars of hope, — dear stars that ever lift —
Until I see home-lights through woodland rift —
The soul from doubt and terror into light.

And now I stand upon the mountain height ;
Below, the valley glimmers to the deep,
Where ships at anchor ride, and sailors sleep.

MY VESTAL LOVE.

MY vestal love, the one eternal light,
　　Who watchest that dim flame within my soul,
Forever fading, yet forever bright,
That it die not, though wildest tempests roll, —
Too quick would passion burn the lamp of life,
While the soft moonlight melts into my room,
If thy sweet peace did not rebuke the strife
That hastes my swift, brief thought to its long tomb.

While thou dost watch, I lose the world in dream;
My room becomes a poet's fairyland;
And in the midnight's soothing sounds I seem
To wander on, holding thy spirit hand.
Guard me, O vestal love, and make me strong
To cast away the things that do thee wrong.

LAMENT.

MARK not your dead with senseless stone ;
    No graven image raise,
To mock at hope. Thy nobler life
    Will be her sweetest praise.

Let not thy wandering steps be led,
    From the joyous world apart, —
Fold the wings of thy heavy grief,
    Close to thy very heart.

Death who hath made thee desolate,
    Hath freed her soul from pain.
Make life more beautiful and true
    For the loves that still remain.

NO DEATH.

IT is not death to die, —
    Though in the sunset's red
Summer lies fair and dead.

It is not death to die, —
Though love's first dream fall dead
Upon its bridal bed.

HER EYES.

DEAR, tender eyes, in which I live,
　　So watchful, willing to forgive,
　　　Sweet, loving eyes,
Deep-set in that too pallid face,
In all its bounds earth holds no place
　　　So close to Paradise.

O faithful eyes, which follow fast,
Raising my spirit, if downcast,
　　　To heaven's brink,
The more I know their wondrous power,
And all their soundless depths, each hour
　　　Deeper in them I sink.

CASTLES IN SPAIN.

BY the stately Guadalquivir
    Many castles towering rise,
Imaged in the dreaming river,
Aiming at the dream-like skies.

Oh ! of all my castles gleaming,
May one tower of thought and prayer,
One white tower, reach up to heaven
Though all others fade in air.

NIGHTFALL.

I LOVE the purpling shadows on the hills
　　Against the crimson sky and earliest star,
The songs of peasants coming from afar,
As happy as the songs of woodland rills;
I love the last rose-blush upon the lake,
When the sun pauses in the glowing West,
And of the earth a last kiss seems to take
Ere he depart and leave the twilight blest.

All these fair sights I love, yet far away
I live from this dear calm, in noisy streets,
Where one can only dream the close of day,
Nor taste of Nature's health-restoring sweets.
Yet are we wont to call sweet freedom ours —
So used to chains we know not half our powers.

HOME-COMING.

WHAT place on earth more lovely than this town,
    Now when the young moon pours its splendor o'er
The dreaming roadway, meadow, and far down
On river winding to the sea? — and more
Than all, it seems, upon this quiet home,
Making it fair without, as love within
Has made it heaven-sweet to one new come
From weary travel and the great world's din.

From room to room I wander like a ghost,
And from each window find some new delight
For eye and soul.   Around me are a host
Of angels sent to bless — what second sight
May one not claim, if he but hold in heart
Most pure and high God's holy gift of art.

SHELLEY.

L ET him lie there, let him lie there beside
     His brother Keats.   Upon his lips, foam-kissed,
Those songs were last when Death's relentless tide
Wound his pale brows about with pallid mist,
Then fled before the strong soul's ardent flame,
Back-driven to the ancient Stygian lair.
Defeated, dumb, and awful in his shame,
Death waits and watches now with vacant stare.

Eternal soul of man, how strong to save !
How strong to live, outlasting Death's great pain !
Remembering Shelley's triumph, we grow brave
To barter life itself for surer gain, —
Since joy beyond all vision rent the night,
When that swift spirit melted into light.

AFTERNOON IN THE CAMPAGNA.

A MASS of golden buttercups thrown in
    By a free hand across this young, sweet field ;
Beyond it all the Sabine Mountains yield
Their purple glow the smiles of heaven to win ;
Here blood-red poppies dance among the wheat,
Through olive-groves are seen the wandering sheep,
The earth yields everything that makes life sweet,
The hours drift by as dreams of placid sleep.

Soft-falling shadows soothe the languid eyes ;
Rome fadeth slowly on the fainting sight,
The mellow distance weds it to the skies,
And Peter's dome swims high in rosy light ;
To one who rests beside this ruined wall
The pulse of God beats music through it all.

WOMAN.

GOD made Hope, and called her Woman —
   Ask thy heart if this be true, —
What so tender as her kisses,
   Falling like the new-born dew?

MARIAE NASCENTI.

SILENT, deathlike, was the city,
 Hidden in a ghostly cloud,
That had crept from Alpine ridges,
 Winding round it like a shroud.

Through the by-ways had I wandered
 Out into the open day,
Where the struggling feet have hollowed
 Stones that pave the ancient way.

Lo ! the Grand Cathedral started
 Like a snow-drift from the mire,
Clad in all her bridal garments,
 Watched by many a stately spire.

And the soothing music drew me
 Gently through the open door,
For my haunted heart was weary,
 Waiting for its " lost Lenore."

Silence all, save my slow footsteps,
 And the Latin monotone,
Chanted back by solemn echoes,
 Dying in the vaults of stone.

Over all, the suffering Saviour
 Hung upon the cruel tree, — .
Pleading: " Wanderer, I was weary.
 Think, oh, think of Calvary ! "

IN FLORENCE.

FLORENCE, city born of flowers,
   Bids me take my lyre again,
Tune it to the rippling Arno,
   Sing this little song to men.

I must play my feeble treble
   In the symphony of spring;
For the swallow is not silent,
   Though he has no voice to sing.

Lyre, befriending hours of sadness
   Passed so oft in mournful song,
When the mind, a wounded eagle
   Droops the wings that once were strong.

E'en the cypress, where the cloister
   Lifts its half-demolished trunk,
Murmurs in a softer cadence
   To the barefoot, shriven monk.

But the student in his attic,
   Where the smoke ascends on high,
Lifts his tired eyes to the mountains,
   And his carol is a sigh, —

Sigh, because he 's bound forever
   With the fetters forged by gold,
And his life is merest barter
   In the mart where lives are sold.

In his window is a flower,
   Gathered on some Sunday's tour ;
This, alas, is all the country,
   All the villa of the poor.

Is this justice? By the river,
   Where the palace lifts its head, —
In the sight of all this splendor, —
   Some one lacks a crust of bread !

Often, often have I asked it
   Of the silent midnight sky,
And the Arno answered only,
   As the student, with a sigh.

AUTUMN.

'NEATH the chestnut the gold leaves are lying,
    Though the sumach still glows with its red ;
But the beauty of summer is dying —
    The soul of the summer is fled.

The old paths no longer are shaded,
    The trees in the forest are bare,
And the ferns, into phantoms faded,
    Are haunting the silence there.

The aster and golden-rod paling,
    Made sadder the meadows' blank face ;
And southward the swallow is sailing —
    Oh, where then, my heart, is thy place ?

THE GRACIOUS DAY.

UNTO the deepening night the day has gone,
  And left its mystery of hope and fears,
That cannot wait the promise of the dawn,
But cry, impatient, to the coming years.

In one man's life this day is shrined apart ;
Earth seemed to him filled with celestial light,
Which flowed through darkened chambers of his heart,
And flowing, lighted them and left them bright.

Shot through and through with this Promethean fire,
Now is he like the spirit of a' star,
That shrivels in its flame all low desire ;
For his true mansion beacons him from far,

And memories of that gracious day are wrought
Into majestic colonnades of thought.

MERCY.

AT last I know that love doth soften law,
  Or else I dare not hope or ask for grace, —
Failing, where I had thought to be so strong,
Even to walk in my accustomed place,
I did not know God's mercy till I fell
From self-made heaven to this, a self-made hell.

UNREST.

OH ! but once to see beyond me,
  Pierce the meshes of the veil,
Once to stand where man has never,
  Just without the earthly pale !

Is this longing all men's birthright
  Since the day when Cain was curst?
Are there here no wells of Lethe
  Deep enough to quench our thirst?

AT THE GATES.

DOWN with your roses into the dust !
　　Let the lips of your song be sealed !
Snatch manhood's sword from the scabbard of rust,
　　And strike till this curse be healed !

Let us hymn no more to Apollo and Pan !
　　What use, in the face of a wrong,
To be wasting the life and the strength of a man
　　In a cowardly, meaningless song?

We are wearing the linen and purple rich,
　　Made of heart, of soul, and of brain,
Of the children who strain, and the women who stitch
　　Till their eyes burn out with pain.

Oh, down with your roses into the dust !
　　Let the lips of your song be sealed !
Awake your sword from its scabbard of rust,
　　And strike till this wrong be healed !

91

THE HOUSE WHERE KEATS DIED.

IN that brown house upon the Spanish Stair
    Keats died, and yet but few of all who go,
Day in and out, along this noisy square,
And up and down these sunny steps, can know
This thing, — or knowing, care to turn aside.
They dream not of the spell about the place,
The balm for aching hearts unsatisfied,
The loveliness a little child might trace.

Rome is to Art more dear for Keats' dear sake;
He found no rest, yet troubled not the fates;
More patient here an exile's home to make.

Although the age oppress, one's spirit waits.
Yet, stones that held this form for whom I sigh,
Tell me what death becomes when such men die!

A CAGED LARK.

IN THE MARKET-PLACE, FLORENCE.

A LARK I found in a dark stall, alone,
  Fast in a cage his fettered wing could span;
Yet sang he as if meadows were his own,
His happy note all jarring sounds outran.
I could have bought the singer; but the song, —
The heart behind the song, — ah ! who could buy?
Shut in by bars and stared at by the throng,
He still was true to his one bit of sky.

What a rich lesson from a lowly place,
And in a tiny thing, the Lord may hide !
The vault of heaven shines down upon my face;
And I dare look it back, dissatisfied.
The whole world for my own, I cannot sing
As this poor tiny bird, this prisoned thing.

IN MEMORIAM.

BE it not mine to question or lament,
　　No storm of grief shall break her songs of praise;
I will not think of shadow-haunted days, —
God does not give to take the joys He sent;
I will not doubt or wrong His dear intent;
Thinking of her, in soul I walk the ways
She walks securely now, — no tangled maze
Of broken hopes or bliss with sorrow bent.

Hers is a joy supreme beyond our thought;
I look at night into the solemn skies,
And for a moment fancy I have caught
Her spirit's calm.　Thank God that one may die
At length and rest, — all battles bravely fought,
All earthly needs and frets laid softly by.

THE OLD MASTERS.

Y E men who broke the way to that new birth,
   'T is not for what ye found, but what is sought,
We love you most; and yet your work is worth,
   Through self-renouncing love, the crown it wrought.
It is the aim, and not the goal we hold
   Most dear,— the thought that lives in tower and stone,
The patient struggle of the spirit bold,
   To wrest some beauty from that dim unknown.

Ye masters old ! men carve in later days
   More perfect statues with their cunning tools.
I would they had your vigor, you their praise,
   Your reverent toil shot through these flippant schools :
Ye carved with faith that makes our vision seem,
   Not holy art, but some irreverent dream.

www.ingramcontent.com/pod-product-compliance
Lightning Source LLC
Chambersburg PA
CBHW020035030726
47499CB00007B/2435